WISE TALES FROM THE EAST

WISE TALES FROM THE EAST

The Essential Collection

Uri Kaplan

Prapañca
Press

First Edition

Prapanca Press.

Library of Congress Cataloging-in-Publication Data

Names: Kaplan, Uri, author.
Title: Wise Tales From the East: The Essential Collection / Uri Kaplan.
Description: Prapanca Press, 2020. | Series: Wise Tales.
Identifiers: LCCN 2020914132 | ISBN 9789655992960 (hardcover) | ISBN 9789659285105 (softcover)
Subjects: Literature (general) — Folk Literature--Fables | Buddhism — Modifications, schools, etc. — Zen Buddhism
Classification: PN980-995 | BQ9250-95

How does one express the ineffable?

Table of Contents

Foreword

ONCE UPON A TIME, as stories often go, a peaceful community of farmers lived in a small village. The hamlet's architecture was distinctive, and the people followed unique customs and maintained long-lasting traditions.

In one particularly hot year, an awful drought hit their village and all the crops withered. The people were hungry. The wise elders assembled for an emergency meeting and sent a delegation to perform the traditional protection ritual. It was done in a secret, magical place in the forest, where they ignited a sacred fire with holy matches and chanted the special prayers. And it worked. Thunder was heard on their way back to the village, and they soon felt drops of rain hit their heads and soak their clothes.

Years and decades passed, births were celebrated and deaths were mourned, until one summer, the neighboring village was preparing to wage war against the community. Everyone was terrified, and the elders again assembled for an emergency meeting. They decided to perform the age-old protection ritual. A delegation set off immediately to the secret place in the forest and ignited the sacred fire with the holy matches. Yet, so many years had passed that no one remembered the special prayers. Nevertheless, the ritual was a success and the war was prevented.

Further years and decades passed, until one winter, a dreadful plague spread through the village. People were dying, and the elders organized an urgent expedition to perform the protection ritual. But when the villagers reached the forest, they realized that they did not possess the holy matches. The matches were apparently lost, buried under the mounds of time. Nevertheless, the mere presence of the delegation at the secret ritual place was enough, and the epidemic was stopped.

Years and decades continued to pass in relative calm, until one memorable winter, persistent rains flooded the entire village. It was still pouring when the elders assembled for an emergency meeting. This time, unfortunately, there was no one left in the entire community who knew where the secret, magical place was, no one who had the holy matches in his possession, and no one who could chant the ancient prayers. But they all still remembered the *story* of the ritual. They retold it all together throughout the night, and in the morning, the rains stopped.

As the fable above illustrates, stories really do seem to contain magical powers. They are able to unite communities, establish identities, and maintain traditions. They can teach, soothe, and inspire people for deeper insights and changed behaviors. Stories can be therapeutic and help us overcome difficult times. They often clarify ideas better than direct explanations. Perhaps, at times, stories are even able to impart the ineffable: that nuanced intuition that is beyond direct speech. But most of all — I think we could all agree — stories can be entertaining and pleasurable.

Many of the great teachers in history used stories, parables, and fables to impart their teachings. Buddhist texts often explain that the Buddha resorted to teaching in parables because the explicit truth was beyond language. Close to half of the stories in this volume were borrowed from the Buddhist tradition. The rest were taken from Daoist (Taoist), Yoga, Hindu, and Confucian texts, as well as from Indian, Chinese, Japanese, and Korean folklore. I allowed myself to play around liberally with some of the stories in order to make them more presentable. A complete list of sources is included at the end of the book for the more scholarly-inclined reader.

The forty-nine wise tales found in this book were not randomly selected. I have used them throughout the years in classes and lectures, and found that they stirred the best reactions from students and friends. I believe that they are the crème de la crème among the enormous number of short fables originating in India and East Asia.

The number forty-nine was not arbitrarily chosen either. It is a distinct typological number in the Buddhist tradition. Following his enlightenment at the age of thirty-one, the Buddha is said to have instructed his students — with the aid of similes and parables — for exactly forty-nine years before passing into Nirvana at the age of eighty. Buddhist mourning rituals are also often performed for forty-nine days, as it is believed that this is the time it takes the soul to reincarnate into a new body.

A number of different life lessons and morals are embodied in the stories below. Some of their messages are clear and straightforward, but others are more abstract, difficult to grasp, and open to multiple interpretations. Rather than seeing them as a weakness, I tend to see these vague messages as great advantages. They are useful tools for inspiring self-reflection and stimulating conversations in classrooms and in therapy sessions. It is thus best to view this book as a resource for public speakers, college professors, teachers, and therapists. A relevant story may be found in it for various occasions.

But this book is certainly not meant for professional use alone. All those interested in the wisdom of the East may find these stories appealing. Hopefully, some readers will find them as mind blowing as I have. I recommend giving each story its due time, patiently mulling it over before moving on to the next tale. After all, stories are a kind of play. They should be engaged with and enjoyed, rather than rushed through absentmindedly. So take your time and read these stories as if you were a child. Read them as if they were true.

This Will Change

WHEN DOJO LEFT home to join the monastery, he was young, eager, and enthusiastic. His mind was determined to sit and meditate for as long as it took to attain enlightenment. Waking up before dawn, he crossed his legs and straightened his back for many hours every day, trying to calm his mind.

A week passed by, and then two. Dojo's knees ached and his back was sore. He was exhausted. He wasn't sure how much longer he could keep this up. Worries and doubts ran through his mind. He couldn't remember why he became a monk in the first place.

As he marched through the garden one day, Dojo came across the head of the monastery. Seeing the old Zen master, he was unable to hold back his frustration. "Nothing is working for me," he blurted. "My legs hurt and I am restless and anxious. This practice is worthless!"

The old Zen master listened quietly to the young monk. He nodded his head in sympathy. "Don't worry," he said. "This will change."

Dojo went back into the meditation hall. He would give it some more time. He counted his breaths and observed his thoughts and emotions. A month passed by, and then two. His body became supple and relaxed. His thoughts settled. Dojo felt much happier.

As he strolled through the garden one day, Dojo encountered the old master again. This time he had good news. "The meditation is finally working!" he exclaimed. "I feel calmer and happier. I think I am getting close!"

The old Zen master listened quietly to the young monk. He nodded his head. "Don't worry," he said. "This will change too."

One Taste

MANY YEARS AGO, two young monks lived in the ancient kingdom of Silla. Wonhyo and Uisang were their names. They were both of noble birth and high aspirations. The greatest Buddhist masters at the time lived in the neighboring kingdom of Tang, and the young monks decided to go study abroad.

At that point in history, there were no trains, buses, or flights. The young monks had to walk. The journey was rough and perilous. They hiked through steep mountains teeming with tigers and snakes. One night, they were caught in a great thunderstorm. They found shelter in a dark cave. Exhausted from the trip, they fell asleep immediately.

Wonhyo woke up in the middle of the night. His throat was dry. He was thirsty. He scrabbled around in the dark and grabbed a gourd. It was brimming with cool, refreshing rainwater. Wonhyo relieved his thirst and went back to sleep.

The storm was gone in the morning. Tiny drops were still dripping from the edge of the cave, but the sun was shining brightly. Wonhyo and Uisang woke up and looked around. This was no ordinary cave, they realized. It was an ancient tomb. Skeletons were scattered all over the ground.

Wonhyo discovered that the gourd he had drank from during the night was a human skull. It was filled with putrid flesh. The young monk was horrified. He bent over and vomited. Then he suddenly stopped.

Wonhyo took a deep breath and started laughing. He could not believe that the disgusting, rotten flesh seemed so refreshing in his mind the previous night. Everything has one taste, he realized. The young monk was now awake. There was no longer any need to seek further study. He said his goodbyes and returned home.

The Poisoned Arrow

MALUNKYAPUTTA SAT IN MEDITATION in the forest. He had heard the instructions of the Buddha and tried to follow them as best he could. Sitting cross-legged, he contemplated the disintegration of bodies and the fickleness of thoughts. But nagging concerns kept running through his mind.

There was still much Malunkyaputta did not understand and the Buddha did not explain. "How old is this world we live in?" he wondered aloud. "Was it created at one point in time, or was it always simply there? And what is the nature of this enlightenment we have been seeking? What would happen to an enlightened person after he or she will eventually die?"

Malunkyaputta could not sit still any longer. He rose from his mat and hastened to the dwelling place of the Buddha. "If you do not know the answers to my questions," he demanded, "the honest thing to do would be to admit it! If that is the case, I have no use for your training and I will go seek a better teacher!"

The Buddha kept his silence for a long while. Finally, he began to speak. "Let me tell you a story, Malunkyaputta," he said. "Imagine a man who has been struck with a poisoned arrow. Surely, he was in great pain. The poison blurred his thoughts. His wife rushed him to the doctor. But the dazed man would not let the doctor operate. 'Before you take out this arrow, I need to know who shot it,' he demanded. 'Was he a tall man or a short one? Was he blond or dark-haired? Where was he from? What was his occupation? Why did he shoot me? And the arrow — was it new or old? Was it made from wood or iron? And from what kind of bird was the feather at its end?'"

"Malunkyaputta," said the Buddha, "as you can imagine, this man would die from his wound before he would be able to find out the answers to these questions. Malunkyaputta, your concerns are similar to those of the injured man. Answering them would not help you. I have explained what needs to be done in order to stop suffering. You must hurry and free yourself from suffering."

Malunkyaputta hustled back to his seat in the forest. He sat cross-legged. The sun was still up. "I can still put in a few more hours of meditation before sleep," he thought.

Forgetting

ANCIENT SAGE ZHUANGZI reclined on his desk, lost in thought.

"The trap is for the rabbit," he considered. "But after I catch the rabbit, I can throw away the trap!"

"Likewise, the net is for the fish," he pondered. "But after I catch the fish, I can throw away the net!"

"In the same way, the words are for the meaning," he mused. "But after I catch the meaning, I can throw away the words!"

Zhuangzi sat in silence. Then he laughed to himself: "I wish I could meet a friend who has already thrown away the words. It would be great to have a word with someone like that!"

A Piggyback Ride

ON A LOVELY sunny day, Dojo accompanied his old master on his alms round. On their way back to the monastery, they had to cross a stream. Preparing to go into the water, they noticed a beautiful woman standing on its bank, crying. She explained that she was in a hurry to return home but was scared to be swept away by the strong current.

Young Dojo averted his eyes. He had taken a vow of celibacy and could not bear to look at the attractive woman. The old master, however, seemed oblivious to his vows. Right away and without a word, he lifted the woman, put her on his back, and carried her across the stream.

The two monks continued walking to their monastery in silence. The young monk was trying to contain his anger. They marched for a long time before he was able to work up the courage to confront his master. "How could you carry that woman on your back?" he demanded. "As monks, we vowed to never touch a woman!"

The old master stopped and looked at his disciple. "I already set the woman down long ago on the other side of the stream," he said softly. "Why are you still carrying her with you?"

The Three Princesses

ONCE UPON A TIME, in a faraway land, lived three happy princesses. But truth be told, they were by no means ordinary princesses. Two of them were never born, and the third was never conceived.

Unfortunately, one day a terrible earthquake destroyed their kingdom. All their relatives died. The poor princesses had to leave their land and look for a new home.

The three princesses marched for days in the desert. Their feet burned in the scorching sand. Exhausted, they stopped to rest in the shade of three trees. Two of the trees were never planted, and the third had no trunk, no branches, and no leaves. After resting for a while and eating the fruit of the trees, they continued on their way.

Eventually, the three princesses reached the banks of three rivers. Two of the rivers were dry, and in the third, there was no water. They bathed cheerfully in the rivers and quenched their thirst. Feeling refreshed, they continued on their way.

Finally, the three princesses reached a great city, one which was about to be built. Three magnificent palaces towered above it. Two of the palaces had no walls, and the third had never been constructed. The three princesses stepped into these lovely palaces and lived happily ever after.

How real are the sad and happy stories that make up our lives?

The Happy Fish

Ancient sage Zhuangzi strolled leisurely with his friend on the banks of the Hao River. He watched the water and smiled. "Look at the little fish jump around and play," he said to his friend. "These fish are really happy!"

Zhuangzi's friend watched the fish and frowned. "You are not a fish," he pointed out to Zhuangzi. "How do you know if the fish are happy?"

But Zhuangzi was no fool. He grinned and replied using the same coin. "You are not me, my friend," he said. "How do you know what I know and what I do not know?"

Zhuangzi's friend sensed that the conversation was getting out of hand. "Let us be rational," he proposed. "Surely I am not you and you are not a fish. This must mean that you do not know if fish are happy!"

Zhuangzi looked at his friend with sympathy and sighed. "Rationality," he said, "would get you nowhere. By asking me 'how do you know if the fish are happy,' you already knew that I know. Well, I know it simply by looking at the Hao River!"

Blowing in the Wind

THE PROMINENT ZEN MASTER Huineng strolled back to his monastery. It was a sunny day, and he enjoyed the open air. When he was approaching the gates, he overheard two young monks arguing about a flag.

The two were looking up at the flag of the monastery blowing in the wind and debating. One of them argued, "It is the flag that is moving!" But the other insisted, "No! It is the wind that is moving!"

The two young monks halted their argument abruptly upon seeing their master. They bowed respectfully and told him about their dispute. "Is it the flag or the wind that is moving?" they asked.

The Zen master smiled knowingly. "It is neither," he said. "It is only your mind that is moving."

The Acrobats

A **SKILLED ACROBAT** balanced on a slender, long bamboo pole. His young protégé Medakathalika struggled to climb the pole and stand on his shoulders. It felt like her hundredth attempt. Halfway up the pole, she kept losing her balance and dropping to the ground along with her teacher.

Medakathalika tried her best to protect her teacher by keeping the pole still and stable. She looked up at him while climbing, making sure he was safe. If she saw him tilt a bit to the right, she attempted to draw her weight to the left. And if she saw him tilt to the left, she drew her weight to the right. But instead of protecting her teacher, her actions made both acrobats collapse on the sand.

They took a break and the skilled acrobat poured his protégé a glass of water. "Medakathalika," he said, "you have to change your focus. Instead of trying to protect me," he suggested, "just watch over yourself. If I watch myself and you watch yourself, we might be able to balance together safely on the long pole."

Medakathalika decided to give it a shot. She concentrated on her own actions, swiftly climbed the bamboo pole, and stood on her teacher's shoulders. Now they were balancing together safely, high off the ground. By watching their own selves, they were able to protect each other.

Hemp

ONCE UPON A TIME, a couple of cloth merchants were traveling on business. Before returning to their homeland, they came across a large pile of abandoned hemp. They decided to make two bundles of hemp and carry them back home with them.

The load was heavy, and the merchants stopped to rest in a small village. There, they noticed an abandoned pile of hemp thread lying around. "This is great!" said one of the merchants. "It is just what we needed the hemp for. Let us leave our bundles of hemp and take some of the hemp thread instead."

But his friend was hesitant. "I have already carried the bundle of hemp this far," he said. "I can't just let go of it now."

Now one of the merchants carried a new bundle of hemp thread, and the other a bundle of hemp. They continued on their journey and stopped for the night in a small town. In the morning, they spotted an abandoned pile of hemp cloth on the corner of the street. "This is great!" exclaimed one of the merchants. "It is just what we needed the hemp for. Let us leave our bundles here and take some new hemp cloth instead!"

But his friend was still doubtful. "I have already carried this bundle of hemp for so long," he sighed. "I can't just leave it here."

Now one merchant was carrying a bundle of hemp cloth, and the other a bundle of hemp. Before reaching their homeland, the weary travelers took a final break in a small hamlet. They were surprised to discover a pile of abandoned gold coins near the gates. "This is amazing!" cried out one of the merchants. "This is just what we needed the hemp for. Let us take the gold instead of our bundles!" Without waiting for an answer, he threw away his bundle of hemp cloth and gathered as many gold coins as he could carry.

But his friend could not be convinced. "I have carried this bundle of hemp with me for the entire trip," he insisted. "We are almost home; I can't just get rid of it."

The Zen Master Who Killed a Cat

IT WAS A PLEASANT autumn day in a prominent ancient Zen monastery. The monks were huddled together, fussing over an endearing cat. Hearing their loud voices, the Zen Master hurried into the hall and grabbed the cat. He held it up in the air and declared: "Monks! If you say a word of truth, I will spare the cat. Otherwise, I will slay the poor animal immediately!"

The monks were shocked and speechless. They could not answer. So the Zen Master killed the cat and left the hall.

That evening, an old monk came to visit the monastery. The Zen Master poured him some tea and told him about the cat incident. The old monk immediately put his sandals on top of his head and walked away.

The Zen Master smiled. "If only the old monk had been there," he thought to himself, "the cat could have been saved!"

Do not hold back.

The Runaway Horse

ONCE UPON A TIME, a simple farmer raised a handsome stallion on his ranch. The sturdy horse helped him plow the fields. But one morning, when he went outside, he discovered that the horse was missing. Someone left the gates open, and the horse ran away. Neighbors came around to offer their sympathies. "What terrible luck," they said.

"Maybe you are right," replied the farmer. "We'll see."

A week passed by. Then one afternoon, the horse suddenly returned, leading several wild mares back to the farm with him. The neighbors rushed over. "What great luck!" they exclaimed. "Now instead of one horse, you have many!"

"Maybe you are right," replied the farmer. "We'll see."

Another week passed by. The farmer's son was trying to tame one of the wild mares, and she flung him violently to the ground. He broke his leg. Neighbors came over again. "What terrible luck," they said.

"Maybe you are right," replied the farmer. "We'll see."

The following week, the National Guard was passing through the village and banging on doors. They were recruiting all able-bodied men to the military. The farmer's son was still recovering from his injury. They let him stay home. Neighbors visited again. "What great luck!" they marveled. "It was all for the best!"

"Maybe you are right," replied the farmer. "We'll see."

Beautiful Flaws

MANY YEARS AGO in ancient China, an old woman walked down to the village well. This was her regular routine. She had walked this road twice a day her entire life to fetch water. A couple of clay pots were dangling from her sides. One of the pots was perfectly formed, and the other was a little cracked.

The cracked pot was always ashamed. Water was dripping from it constantly, and when the old woman arrived home, it was always only half full. But she did not replace it.

One day, as the woman was walking back from the well, the cracked pot could not bear the humiliation any longer. It was wet and messy and dripping all over the road. "Why do you keep using me for water?" it asked in frustration. "I am flawed and useless. Why don't you just replace me?"

The old woman smiled at the cracked pot. "Look down at the ground," she said to it softly.

The cracked pot obliged. It was surprised to discover beautiful flowers blooming only on its side of the road. They formed a lovely path all the way down to the well. Unknowingly, he had been watering them for years.

The woman picked up a couple of lilies from the side of the road to decorate her simple home.

A Handful of Mustard Seeds

ONCE UPON A TIME in ancient India, a young woman gave birth to an adorable baby. She raised him cheerfully and loved him dearly. Unfortunately the child was ill, and a year later, he died.

The young woman was struck with grief. She could not let go of her son. Weeping and moaning, she held him in her arms and traveled from door to door seeking a cure. She needed medicine that would bring her son back to life.

Of course no one could obtain such medicine for her. But the woman would not give up. As she was walking in the village one day, she encountered the Buddha and told him her sad story.

The Buddha listened quietly to the sorrowful woman. "There may be one way to solve your problem," he finally said. "In order to concoct a potion that would bring your son back to life, you must obtain a handful of mustard seeds from a house where no one has lost a child, a parent, a spouse, or a friend," he explained. "Once you get such seeds, bring them over to me and I will cure your baby."

The young woman was invigorated with new hope. She rushed from house to house in search of a family that had never known a death. But she could not find one. Each family she visited recounted its own unfortunate experience with death. The woman gradually became weary. She sat on the side of the road and watched the dimming lights of the village. She was now ready to go bury her son.

Help the Grain

SPIRITS WERE LOW at the rice farm. People were starving. The rains were late this year, and the sprouts were still small. There was not much left to eat.

Song was hungry and concerned. He decided to take action. The following day he woke up early and left the house in a hurry. In the evening, he returned filthy and exhausted. "Today I helped the grains grow!" he announced in front of everyone.

The farmers all ran out to take a look. They could not believe Song's stupidity. The grains were all plucked, torn, and withered. It was hopeless. Surely, no one can rush time.

The Nature of Scorpions

DOJO AND HIS FRIEND were sitting on the bank of the stream. The two monks had just finished their midday meal. They stepped out to wash their bowls. As they sat quietly side by side and scrubbed, they noticed a small scorpion drowning in the water. Dojo reached out his hand and grabbed it. He placed the scorpion safely on the bank of the stream and let out a slight shriek. "Ouch," he cried. "The scorpion stung me."

The two monks went on scrubbing their bowls quietly. But soon the scorpion stumbled back into the stream. It was drowning again. Dojo reached out his hand and placed the scorpion on safe ground. "Ouch," he cried out again. "The scorpion stung me."

Dojo's hand ached, but the two monks went on scrubbing their bowls. Before they knew it, the clumsy scorpion fell into the water again. Dojo grabbed it once more and placed it on the ground. "Ouch," he cried out yet again. "The scorpion stung me."

Now Dojo's friend was annoyed. "Why do you keep grabbing the scorpion?" he scolded. "Can't you see that it just stings you over and over again? It doesn't care if you are trying to save it! Stinging is the nature of scorpions. They just can't help it!"

Dojo kept scrubbing his bowl. He looked at his friend. "Stinging may be the nature of scorpions," he said to him finally. "But compassion is the nature of monks."

The Benefits of Uselessness

1

ANCIENT SAGE ZHUANGZI was deep in thought when he suddenly heard a knock on his door. His friend barged in all grumpy. He was complaining before Zhuangzi even had time to pour him a drink.

"The king presented me with expensive seeds for huge gourds," he told Zhuangzi. "I was excited at first, but the gourds they produced were simply too big. I tried using them as water containers, but they became too heavy to lift. I tried using them as dippers, but they were too big to fit into anything. They were practically useless, so I smashed them to pieces!"

Zhuangzi urged his friend to drink up. "You really are dumb," he teased him amicably. "You had such fantastic gourds and you worried about them being useless for such trivial matters. There are greater uses for the useless. Why didn't you just climb into one of the gourds and go floating leisurely on the rivers and lakes?"

2

The following week, Zhuangzi paid a visit to his friend. They sat on his porch and stared at an enormous old tree in the garden.

"This tree is so twisted and rotten I can't make anything out of it," Zhuangzi's friend ranted. "It is impossible to make tables or beds out of it, and no carpenter is willing to buy it from me," he added. "I should just cut it down and get rid of it."

"Well," replied Zhuangzi, "you really never learn, do you?" He gulped down his wine. "You have such a fantastic tree, but you are worried about it being useless for making furniture. Why don't we just go and rest in its shade, or simply lie down and take a nap under its broad canopy?"

Mountains Are Mountains

WHEN DAOCHUAN WAS a young man during the Song Dynasty, he liked to take long walks in the forest. He enjoyed hiking alone, immersed in nature. At the time, he perceived things in a simple way. He saw the mountains as mountains and the rivers as rivers. Things were naturally as they were.

Years later, Daochuan ended up shaving his head and joining a Zen monastery. He practiced meditation and achieved some insight. Gradually he started perceiving things differently. Mountains were no longer mountains, and rivers were no longer rivers.

Daochuan was getting older. Finally, one cloudy day, he achieved a great awakening. Comfortably relaxed in his seat, he looked around.

Now he perceived the mountains as just mountains and the rivers as just rivers.

But is there a difference between the three perspectives?

The Blind Men and the Elephant

MANY YEARS AGO in ancient India, a strange animal was brought to town for the first time. It was called an elephant. The curious residents all gathered around to take a closer look. Among them was a group of blind men.

The blind men could not see the large animal. They had to inspect it by touch. They approached it cautiously from all sides, groping its body.

"It's a thick snake, like an anaconda!" cried out one of the blind man. He groped the twisting trunk of the elephant and jumped back in fear. "Be careful!" he warned his friends.

"Come on," said a second blind man. "Don't you realize that it is just like a large fan?" He groped one of the flapping ears of the elephant. He stood next to it, enjoying the cool breeze.

"There is nothing to be alarmed about," he concluded.

"What are you two talking about?" said a third blind man. He was holding one of the legs of the elephant. "This animal is just like a thick pillar," he claimed, "steady and unmoving."

A fourth blind man was holding the tail of the elephant. "Have you all lost your senses?" he yelled out. "This animal is just like a rope. We can use it to tie things up."

The blind men kept arguing for hours. But none of them knew the real shape of the elephant. Which one of the blind men are you?

Empty Your Cup

ONCE UPON A TIME, a learned professor decided to visit a Buddhist monastery. He asked the abbot to teach him about Zen. The kind monk agreed and invited the professor into his chambers.

They sat down in a small room. As the monk prepared tea in silence, the professor chatted away. He talked about Buddhist history and philosophy. He spoke of ideas and concepts. He showed true erudition.

In the meantime, the water boiled and the monk started pouring tea into the professor's cup. He poured the tea slowly until it reached the brim of the cup, and then kept on pouring. The professor stopped talking and watched the overflowing cup. The tea was spilling to the floor, but the monk kept on pouring it into the full cup.

Eventually, the professor could not hold it in any longer. "It's full!" he blurted. "No more tea can go in it!"

The monk stopped pouring tea into the full cup. He looked at the professor. "How can I fill your mind with Zen," he asked, "if your mind is already full?"

A Feast for a Bird

AN EXTRAORDINARY BIRD was nesting at the shores of the ancient state of Lu. Its colors were spectacular, and it sang each morning in a lovely voice that attracted the crowds. It soon drew the attention of the king, who ordered to have the bird brought to the palace.

Once he laid his eyes on the exquisite bird, the king was captivated. He decided to throw an extravagant feast in its honor, one usually reserved only for great kings. His cooks prepared the most refined dishes, and musicians performed the most sophisticated melodies. The king and his attendants enjoyed themselves greatly.

But the bird seemed dazed and distressed. It fluttered in circles restlessly inside the hall, frightened by the sound of the music and barely touching the abundant food. After three days, the bird died.

The king was upset. He had tried to nourish the lovely bird the same way he wanted himself to be nourished, only to end up killing it. He should have known better. He could have simply let it fly freely above the forests and seas.

Most men regarded Lady Li to be of unequal beauty. But when fish saw her, they dove into the deep; when birds saw her, they soared into the skies; and when deer saw her, they ran away without looking back.

Ask the Horse

DOJO WAS SITTING quietly on the side of the road. Suddenly a man riding a horse came galloping through at full speed, almost running over him. Dojo was upset. He jumped to his feet and yelled at the rider:

"Hey! Where are you going in such a hurry and without considering those around you?"

"I really don't know," apologized the man. "Ask the horse!"

Dojo sat back down and reflected. "Am I in control of my mind, or is it my mind that is leading me?" he wondered.

The Opposite Direction

THE KING OF WEI planned to attack the Kingdom of Yue. Wise Minister Liang did not approve of this and rushed to the palace. He bowed to the king and said:

"On my way here, I encountered a man riding his chariot at full speed to the north. He said he was going to Chu."

"'If you wish to go to Chu, why are you heading north?' I asked him."

"'I have fine horses; they can take me there fast,' the man answered."

"'Your horses sure look great,' I told him, 'but this is not the road to Chu.'"

"'But I have a strong, courageous charioteer,' he insisted."

"'Although your driver seems decent, he is going the wrong way,' I told him."

"'But still, I have lots of money and provisions for the journey,' the man argued."

"'I am glad to hear that you lack nothing,' I told him, 'but Chu is simply in the opposite direction!'"

"Your majesty," said Minister Liang. "I hear that you are planning to attack Yue. I realize your resources allow it. But are you sure that would be the right direction?"

The Rivalry of the Faculties

ONE DAY THE SENSE FACULTIES started quarreling with one another. Each of them thought it was superior to the others. Speech, hearing, smell, breath, and thought all boasted their higher significances.

Finally, they decided to ask the Creator who was best among them. And sure enough, the Creator found a quick way to solve their dilemma. "He by whose departure the body suffers the most — he is superior!" he proclaimed.

Upon hearing these words, the tongue decided to leave the body. It stayed away for an entire year. When it returned, it asked the other faculties how they managed without it. "Well, it wasn't easy to live without speaking," they admitted, "but we managed."

The ears departed next. They were gone for two whole years. But when they returned, the other faculties were doing just fine. "It was difficult to live without hearing," they said, "but we managed."

The same occurred when the nose left and returned after three years. The other faculties managed to live without smelling.

It was harder when the mind left. Once it finally returned after four years away, the other faculties confessed: "We lived like a small child whose mind is not yet formed. It was sure difficult to live without thought. But we managed."

Last of all, the breath was preparing to depart. But before it was able to leave, the other faculties gathered up and begged it to stay. "We will not be able to manage without you," they confessed. "We are all grounded in you," they pleaded. "Please stay!"

And that is the reason we always return to the breath.

Learning Swordsmanship

MITSUYOSHI WAS BORN to a prominent samurai family. When he came of age, he sought out the most skilled swordsman in Nara in order to learn the craft from him. He was directed to an old master who lived alone at the edge of town. When he reached his residence, he bowed to the master and asked: "Would you teach me the art of the sword?"

"If you work diligently, I will teach you," agreed the old master. "But you must know that it may take a very long time, perhaps even the rest of your life!"

The young samurai was discouraged. "I can't wait that long!" he cried. "You have never seen a person more hardworking than I am," he promised. "I will serve you and train day and night!"

"I see," said the master. "Well, then perhaps we would be able to finish your training in ten years."

But the young samurai was still disgruntled. "That is still too long," he muttered. "I promise I will train intensively and without rest!" he said.

"In that case," replied the old master, "your training will take thirty years! A man in a hurry never learns quickly," he added.

Where Is the Mind?

BODHIDHARMA WAS A SEVERE Indian Zen Master. He walked all the way from his native land to China and sat cross-legged in a dark cave facing the wall. Huike heard about the famous master and rushed from afar to seek his teachings. He cut off his arm and presented it to Bodhidharma. "Please accept this earnest offering and pacify my anxious mind!" he begged.

Bodhidharma did not move. He seemed indifferent. "Bring me that mind of yours, and I will pacify it for you!" he finally barked.

Huike was speechless. He walked out of the cave lost in thought. After a while, he stepped back in. "I have searched for my mind everywhere but could not take a hold of it!" he said.

"Now your mind is pacified!" answered Bodhidharma, and continued gazing at the wall.

Cook Ding

THE KING WATCHED Cook Ding prepare dinner. It was a marvelous sight. The cook chopped and sliced, grilled and fried, as though he was performing an elaborate dance. He handled his knife as if playing a musical instrument.

"Bravo!" cried out the king. "How did you manage to attain such impressive skills?" he asked.

"When I first started carving beef," recalled the cook, "I saw nothing but the entire ox in front of me. Over the years, I gradually learned to more closely observe the particular parts I was cutting. Nowadays, however, I see the ox with my mind and not with my eyes. I let go of my senses and allow my hands to move naturally through the flesh, the tendons, and the joints of the animal."

"A good chef uses his knife carefully and replaces it only once a year," added the cook. "A mediocre chef replaces his knife once a month because he slashes with it carelessly. But I have had this knife for nineteen whole years and carved thousands of oxen with it," he bragged. "And its blade is still as sharp as if it just came from the grindstone!"

"Excellent!" said the king, and retreated to his chambers. Later, as he was devouring his dinner, he pondered to himself: "I wish I could handle life the same way Cook Ding handles his knife!"

The Tiger's Tail

YEARS AGO IN ANCIENT KOREA, a man was traveling north to the capital. The trip was long and strenuous, and the man decided to take a break. He stretched out under a tree, placed his staff next to him, and took a nap.

Before long, the man woke up and groped for his staff. But as soon as he clutched it, he realized his mistake. Instead of his staff, he was holding the tail of a sleeping tiger.

The man knew he shouldn't move. After all, it wouldn't be wise to wake up a tiger. He kept clutching the tail tightly. He was trapped. He couldn't leave, and it was only a matter of time before the tiger awakened.

After what seemed like a very long time, a stranger finally passed by. "Help!" the man whispered. "Would you mind killing this tiger for me?" he begged. "You can use my staff to beat it."

But the stranger refused to help. "How can I kill an innocent animal?" he reasoned. "I wouldn't be able to live with myself."

The man was noticeably annoyed. He thought for a minute and came up with a solution. "Don't leave," he pleaded. "Why don't we just switch places? You can hold the tail, and I will kill the tiger," he offered.

The stranger agreed. He took hold of the tiger's tail carefully and waited for the man to kill it. But the man walked away. "How can I kill an innocent animal?" he shrugged, leaving the terrified stranger behind.

The Chariot

THE KING WELCOMED a Buddhist monk into his palace and asked him for his name. "My friends call me Nagasena," answered the monk. "But that is merely a name. Let me assure you that there is no person standing here in front of you!"

The king was amused. "If there is no person here," he said, "then who is the one who talks, eats, and wears the monk's robes?"

But the wise monk could not be fazed. "Do you usually travel on foot or by chariot?" he asked the king.

"I travel in the royal chariots, of course," answered the king.

"I see," said Nagasena. "But what are these chariots?" he asked. "Are they the wheels?"

"Of course not," said the king.

"Are they the axles?"

"Of course not," said the king.

"Are they the frame? The screws? The chains? The seats?"

"Of course not," said the king.

"Then there are no chariots!" concluded Nagasena. "Chariots are only designations of other elements but have no independent existence!"

The king was lost in thought. "I suppose you are right," he finally said. "There are no chariots…"

"Now you see," said Nagasena, "in the same way, there is no person standing here in front of you."

Happy Dogs

LONG AGO IN A SMALL Japanese village stood a magnificent magical house. It was made of a thousand mirrors.

One day a little dog decided to visit the magical house. The dog skipped happily into the doorway, wagging his tail. He was pleasantly surprised to discover a thousand other happy dogs wagging their tails around him. He smiled, and a thousand other dogs smiled back at him. The little dog was overjoyed. "That was truly a great house!" he thought to himself on the way back.

The little dog told his friends about the magnificent house, and before long, another dog decided to go and take a look. This dog had a bad day and was gloomy and irritated. He staggered wearily into the doorway, and a thousand dogs were watching him angrily, exposing their teeth. He barked in fear, and a thousand other dogs growled back at him. He was terrified. "What a horrible house!" he thought to himself, as he ran away as fast as he could.

The Jewel in the Pocket

ONCE UPON A TIME, a poor vendor was selling onions in a dusty Indian bazaar. One day, an old school friend passed through the market. He was glad to bump into his old buddy and invited him for dinner at his house.

The house was luxurious, and it seemed that the old friend had done very well for himself. Dinner was superb and drinks were plentiful. Before he knew it, the exhausted vendor got drunk and fell into a stupor.

The host woke up early in the morning. He had business out of town and had to catch the early train. His friend was still passed out on the couch. He did not want to wake him, but he wanted to share some of his wealth with his unfortunate friend. He kindly fetched one of his priceless jewels, placed it in his friend's coat pocket, and left.

The vendor woke up around noon. He grabbed his coat and returned to the bazaar. He did not think to look into his pockets and kept making a meager living by selling onions.

Months passed by, and then years. Poverty took a toll on the vendor's physical and mental health. Then one day, his wealthy old friend returned to the market. He was surprised to see the vendor still sitting on the ground, filthy clothes hanging from his emaciated body. "Look in your pockets!" he cried out immediately.

The vendor found the jewel in his pocket. He realized he had been rich all along. He had all he needed, but he simply neglected to see it. He bought a small house and lived a comfortable peaceful life.

Look in your pockets!

Fart

FAMOUS SONG DYNASTY poet Su Shi sat in meditation near the river. He felt inspired and wrote a short poem:

> *I bow my head to the Heaven of Heavens,*
> *Rays of light illuminate the Great Many,*
> *The winds of honor and disgrace do not shake me,*
> *As I sit still on a golden lotus.*

Satisfied with himself, Su Shi had his poem sent to his friend, the great Zen master Foyin, who lived across the river. But Foyin was unimpressed. Smiling to himself, he simply jotted the word "fart" on the manuscript and sent it back to the poet.

Su Shi was stunned. He knew his friend was not inclined to flattery, but he did not expect such scorn. "How dare this old monk insult me like that?" he fumed. "I must go and confront him!"

Su Shi crossed the river and marched toward the Zen master's hermitage to demand an apology. But the house was empty and the door locked. However, there was a small note on the gate. It read:

> *The winds of honor and disgrace do not shake you,*
> *But one fart blows you across the river!*

The heated poet felt as if he had been sprayed with cold water. It was too early to boast. He went back across the river and sat quietly in meditation.

The Centipede

A GREEN FROG sat on a rock and watched a centipede walking along the bushes. She could not believe her eyes. A hundred legs! What amazing body control! Each leg steps in the right spot at the right time, and the centipede moves rapidly without a worry in the world.

"Hey centipede," the curious frog finally called out. "How do you do that? How do you manage to walk so nimbly with so many legs, without any of them bumping into each other, without tripping or stumbling on your own feet?"

The centipede stopped and stared blankly at the frog. "I never really thought about that," he said. "I guess I just lift each leg at a time and step it forward. It just comes naturally to me."

The centipede was lost in thought. He deliberated, calculated, and considered the movement of his limbs. But when he tried to start walking again, something was off. His numerous legs got tangled up, kicking one another, stepping on each other's feet. Finally, something that never happened before took place. The confused centipede tripped and fell to the ground.

A Line of Candles

One cloudy day, the king summoned the respected monk Nagasena to his palace. He was pondering life and wanted to consult the wise master. "Am I the same person I was when I was a child?" he inquired.

"That is a very wise question," answered the monk. "What does your gut tell you?"

"Well," said the king after a short pause, "the body was obviously different back then, and so was the mind. But it seems like there was something that remained the same all along."

"That is close to the truth," Nagasena nodded. "But in fact, you are neither the same nor different from that child long ago."

"How is it possible to be neither the same nor different?" asked the confused king.

"Allow me illustrate it for you," offered the monk. "Imagine a long line of colorful candles. The first candle in the line is used to light up the second candle, the second candle is used to light up the third candle, the third is used to light up the fourth, and so on until all candles are lit."

"Now what do you think, great king? Is the fire that lights up the first candle the same or different from the fire that lights up the second candle? Is it the same or different from the fire that lights up the last candle?"

Five-Hundred Maidens

BUDDHA'S COUSIN, NANDA, was having difficulties adjusting to the monastic life. He was haunted by the memories of his beautiful wife sleeping calmly by his side. "I intend to renounce the monastic vows and return home," he told his friends.

When the Buddha heard about his cousin's qualms, he decided to pay him a visit. After greeting him kindly, he held his arm, and poof! They both appeared up in heaven.

In heaven, the two cousins witnessed five-hundred gorgeous maidens dancing in the woods. Nanda could barely control his desire for them. "Aren't these maidens more attractive than the wife you left home?" asked the Buddha. "Of course they are," Nanda agreed. "Well then, dear cousin, I promise you that if you meditate earnestly, you will be able to eventually marry these five-hundred gorgeous maidens!"

Once the two cousins landed back on Earth, Nanda immediately ran off to meditate. His motivation was now firm, and he sat cross-legged, striving day and night. The other monks all criticized his goal as unworthy. They called him a fraud, a heretic, and a dirty scumbag. But nothing would shake Nanda now. His goal was clear, and his determination rock solid. He meditated persistently without rest.

Then suddenly, one afternoon, the meditation bore fruit and Nanda was enlightened. The Buddha came over to congratulate his cousin. "Let me now award you the five-hundred maidens I promised," he said. But Nanda shook his head. "There is no need for that any longer," he said quietly.

Why We Shout

AN EMINENT INDIAN GURU went down to wash in the Ganges River with his disciples. At the banks of the river, they noticed a family shouting at each other. The guru turned to his disciples and asked them, "Why do you think this family is yelling so loudly?"

"They are probably shouting because they are angry," the disciples answered.

"But they are standing so close to one another," the guru pointed out. "Do they need to shout to be heard?"

"Of course not," agreed the disciples. "It is rather strange that we shout when we get angry."

"The reason we shout when we get angry," explained the guru, "is not because we are standing far away from one another, but because our hearts are growing farther apart. The angrier we become, the farther apart our hearts get, and our voices have to cover that distance. That is why we shout."

"Love, however, is the exact opposite," continued the guru. "When we love, our hearts grow closer, and all we have to do is whisper to be heard," he explained. "Sometimes our love is boundless and our hearts are so close that we do not need to speak at all. We can simply look into each other's eyes."

The disciples nodded in agreement. This did make a lot of sense.

"When families fight," concluded the guru, "they should not let their hearts get too far apart. Otherwise, one day their hearts will be so distant that they will not be able to hear each other at all."

Empty Boat

"WHY THE LONG FACE?" sage Zhuangzi asked one of his disciples, who was sitting in a corner all by himself.

"I always get criticized by others," complained the young student. "People keep getting angry at me."

"Well," said Zhuangzi, "perhaps I can help. Imagine a man crossing a river on a boat, when suddenly another boat bumps into his vessel violently. The man would obviously get angry and shout and curse at the men in the other boat, wouldn't he?"

"Sure," agreed the student.

"But if the other boat was empty," Zhuangzi continued, "even a severely bad-tempered man would not be able to get mad at it, to yell and swear at it."

"I suppose that's true," said the student.

"Now, if you do not want anyone to get angry at you or do you harm," instructed the sage, "all you have to do is simply empty your own boat. That way, you will be able to roam freely without opposition on the rivers of life."

Four Wives

ONCE UPON A TIME, there was a wealthy man with four wives. The man was old, and his health deteriorating. He knew his time of death was near. Overwhelmed with loneliness, he asked his first wife to accompany him to death.

"I know you always loved and cared for me," answered the first wife, "but I cannot accompany you to death. This is the time to say goodbye."

The disappointed man approached his second wife. "Would you accompany me to death?" he asked.

"I appreciate that you always courted me and held on to me tight, "said the second wife. "But I cannot accompany you to death. I must remain in this world."

Lying on his deathbed, the lonely old man called for his third wife. Perhaps she would agree to accompany him to death.

"You were always important to me," said the third wife," but I cannot accompany you to death. I will go visit you often in the graveyard," she promised.

The frustrated old man called for his fourth wife. He had never paid much attention to her and treated her like a slave. But now he was desperate.

The fourth wife, however, agreed immediately. "I will accompany you wherever you go," she promised. "We will never be separated."

"Now who are these four wives?" asked the Buddha. And explained:

"The first wife is the body. The man loved it and took care of it his whole life, but it couldn't escort him to death."

"The second wife is wealth. The man pursued it and held on to it tightly all his life, but it couldn't go with him to death either."

"The third wife is the family. They could stand by the man throughout his life, but upon death, they could only accompany him as far as the graveyard."

"And the fourth wife is the man's karma. For only the consequences of his beneficial and harmful deeds will follow him forever."

Can't Get No Satisfaction

MANY YEARS AGO, a poor Chinese stonecutter was thrashing his hammer at a rock, panting and sweating from the blazing sun. He was tired of his arduous profession and dreamed of a better destiny. "I wish I was the sun," he thought to himself. "After all, the sun is the most powerful thing in the world and nothing could stand against it."

In an instant, the stonecutter magically turned into the sun. He shined brightly and felt wonderful. But soon, a large cloud floated before him and blocked his luster. "I wish I was a cloud," he thought to himself. "It seems that clouds are even more powerful than the sun!"

Before he could even finish this thought, he magically turned into a huge white cloud. He floated happily in the great blue skies. But before he knew it, a gust of wind blew over and scattered him. "I wish I was the wind," he thought. "It is even more powerful than the clouds!"

His wish was granted again, and he instantly transformed into the wind. He dashed here and there, puffing at trees, twirling leaves, and shaking the waters. Until one day he blew against a rock, and the rock did not move. "I wish I was a rock," he now thought. "It turns out that rocks are the most powerful things!"

This time he magically turned into a rock. He stood still and steady, slowly letting the years pass by. Until one day, a sturdy stonecutter came by and began to pound at it with his hammer. The stunned rock cracked and crumbled. "I wish I was a stonecutter," he thought to himself.

A Skull for a Pillow

ANCIENT SAGE ZHUANGZI was strolling in the forest when he suddenly noticed an old skull. It was lying in the dirt all dried up. He poked at it with a stick and asked: "Dear sir, how did you reach such a wretched state? Was it because of greed or envy? Was it because of war or the punishment of kings? Was it because of hunger or thirst, the heat or the cold? Or was it simply because the years piled up beneath you?"

Since the skull did not reply, Zhuangzi took it with him. When he lay down to sleep in the evening, he tucked it under his head as a pillow.

Late at night, the skull approached him in a dream. "You chatter like a living being but know nothing of the world of the dead!" it told him. "Here there is no greed or envy, no kings and punishments, no hunger or cold, and time simply does not end."

Sleeping Zhuangzi found the words of the skull hard to believe. "Come on!" he said. "We both know that if you had a chance to return to life again, you would do it in a second!"

But the skull just frowned. "Why would I throw away this happiness for the troubles of living beings again?" it muttered. At that moment Zhuangzi woke up.

The Wooden Idol

ONCE UPON A TIME, there was a Buddhist hermit who sculpted a Buddha out of wood. He paid all the money he had for the timber and spent months cutting and polishing it. He wanted the image to look just right. It was as tall as a small building, magnificently shaped, and painted in vivid colors.

The hermit was pleased. He placed the wooden idol in a large hall and sat down in front of it. Gazing at the statue of the Buddha, he began to meditate.

Months passed by, and then years. Finally, one winter day, the hermit was enlightened. He opened his eyes. It was freezing cold. He lit a match and set fire to the wooden Buddha. Now it was warm.

Once you cross the river, you can put down your raft.

Hanging from a Cliff

WHEN A MAN SUDDENLY spotted a tiger in the forest, he did what any of us what do. He ran as fast as he could.

He sprinted, with the tiger chasing after him, until he reached the edge of a gigantic cliff. Not sure what to do next, he grabbed a dangling root and lowered himself under the edge of the rock. Glancing down, he realized that terrifying crocodiles were waiting at the bottom.

The man was now hanging from a steep cliff with a tiger circling above and crocodiles waiting below. And if that wasn't enough, he soon heard peculiar scratching sounds. A rat was gnawing at the root he was holding. He knew he didn't have much time left.

The man exerted all his strength to hold on to the dangling root. He was breathing hard and sweating when he suddenly felt a sting, and then another. Buzzing bees surrounded him. They stung his bare flesh mercilessly.

The man looked up and discovered where the bees were coming from. A large beehive was attached to the cliff right above his head. Small drops of honey were dripping from it.

The man opened his mouth. The honey tasted so sweet that the man forgot all his troubles. He forgot that he was hanging from a cliff and that his time was short. He forgot the tiger, the crocodiles, and the aching bee stings. All he wanted was a little more honey.

"Such is our human existence," said the Buddha. "We constantly endure all sorts of pain and suffering and know that our lives are bound to end soon enough. But we forget all of that in an instant due to a few drops of honey."

The Servant's Dream

MR. YIN WAS A WEALTHY man who owned plenty of servants. His responsibilities were numerous, and he worked his servants without rest from morning to night.

One of Mr. Yin's servants seemed to have always maintained his good spirits. Despite his old age and feeble body, he toiled all day long with a smile on his face. The increasingly annoyed Mr. Yin finally summoned him to inquire what he was grinning about.

"I work all day long and then sleep like a log at night," explained the servant. "When I sleep, I dream that I am a great king, comfortably enjoying the pleasures of the senses," he added. "I wake up to be a servant again, but I am happy as a king whenever I shut my eyes, which is almost half of my time on Earth. Isn't this good enough reason to smile?"

Mr. Yin dismissed the old servant. He was too busy to converse for long. His mind was restless with plans and worries all day long. And on top of that, he knew that when he finally goes to sleep at night, he dreams that he is a servant doing menial work and subjected to all kinds of abuse.

What a shame! Mr. Yin spent half of his life troubled and anxious, and the other half as a lowly servant.

The Mouse King

SAGE YAJNAVALKYA WAS BATHING in the Ganges River when a mouse suddenly fell from an eagle's beak right into his arms. The sage immediately used his magical powers and transformed the mouse into a baby girl. He took her home and raised her.

The girl grew up to be a self-assured, pretty young woman. When she reached the age of marriage, prominent suitors lined up.

First came the Sun King and asked for her hand. But the young woman refused. "He is just too hot for me," she explained.

Second came the Mountain King and asked her to marry him. But she refused again. "He is just too rigid," she apologized.

Then the Wind King arrived. But the young woman rejected him too. "He is just too erratic," she reasoned.

Powerful suitors continued to drop by, but the young woman rejected them all with various pretenses. Until one day, the small grayish Mouse King stood timidly at her door. Hearing of the woman's reputation, he did not expect to have much luck. But she took a long look at him and felt at ease. "He is of my own kind," she felt. She bent down to him and said: "yes!"

The Hawk and the Clam

A LARGE CLAM was basking in the sun, its shell wide open. A hawk spotted it and dove down. It pecked at the clam's flesh, and the angry clam shut its shell and gripped the hawk's beak.

"Let go!" yelled the hawk. "If it does not rain today and it does not rain tomorrow, you will be a dead clam!" warned the trapped hawk.

"Sure," replied the clam. "But if you do not free yourself today and you do not free yourself tomorrow, you will be a dead hawk!" warned the clam.

The stubborn animals argued for hours without giving in. Finally a fisherman walked by and caught them both. He had them for dinner.

The Gates of Heaven

IN MEDIEVAL JAPAN lived a fierce samurai who was terrified of going to hell. His name was Nobushige. He decided to go visit famous Zen Master Hakuin and inquire about heaven and hell. "Do these places really exist?" he asked the old master.

"And who are you?" asked Hakuin.

"Well, I am a renowned samurai of the Takeda clan," answered Nobushige. "Have you not heard of me?"

"You? A renowned samurai?" laughed Hakuin. "Why would anyone hire you as a soldier? You look as weak and feeble as a street beggar!"

The stunned samurai was furious. "How dare the old man talk to me this way?" he raged. As he was about to draw out his sword and slice off the head of the old monk, Hakuin remarked, "Now you are standing at the gates of hell!"

Nobushige stopped and placed his sword back in its sheath upon hearing the words Hakuin. He understood the deep teaching of the old master. He bowed down respectfully and apologized wholeheartedly. "Please forgive my brazenness," he said.

Hakuin smiled. "Now you are standing at the gates of heaven," he said.

The Magic Stick

ONCE UPON A TIME, there was a poor Indian woman who lived with her only child. Ever since he was a little boy, her son had dreamed of playing the flute, but she could not afford one. One day, as the mother was begging for alms, she encountered an old man who gave her a stick of wood. "This stick sure is not much," the old man admitted. "But it may have some magic in it."

The woman reluctantly carried the useless stick back home and gave it to her son. He did not have any toys and was happy to go out and play with the stick. Outside, he saw a man trying to light a fire in his stove. But the firewood was damp from the rain, and he could not cook his meal. The generous boy offered the man his wooden stick, and soon the stove heated up and the meal was ready. He gave the boy some rice and curry.

The boy kept wandering off in the neighborhood until he heard a baby cry. "He is hungry, but I have nothing to feed him," explained his despondent mother. She was selling old clothes from a cart on the side of the road. The boy did not think twice. He took out his rice and curry and offered them to the hungry baby. The grateful mother gave the boy some nice clothes.

Heading down to the river, the boy suddenly encountered a man standing in his underwear next to a horse. "I was robbed of all my money and clothes," explained the strange-looking man. "All I have left is this horse." The boy felt sorry for the poor man and gave him the nice clothes he had just received. The thankful man gave him his horse in return.

Riding the horse back home, the boy came across a wedding hall. The band was sitting outside the building looking depressed. "We were fired," they explained. "The hosts expected majestic musicians riding elephants or horses, but we are poor and only have our instruments with us." The benevolent boy stepped down from the horse and gave it to the musicians. "Thank you!" they exclaimed. "You really saved us! Here, please accept one of our flutes in return."

The Lazy Parrot

ONCE UPON A TIME, a king received two beautiful parrots as a gift. He placed them on a tree outside his palace windows and summoned the royal bird trainer. "Please coach the parrots to fly on command," he instructed.

The trainer worked with the parrots for several weeks and returned to the king. "I was able to train one of the parrots to fly high on command, but the other simply refuses to leave its branch," he said. "Perhaps the bird is unhealthy."

Upon hearing this, the disappointed king summoned various specialized doctors, healers, and trainers from all over the kingdom. They rubbed ointments, concocted medications, and even attempted to use magic spells, but to no avail. The parrot would not budge from its branch. "Maybe the bird is just too lazy," thought the king.

He was about to give up when one of his gardeners, a poor illiterate fellow from the countryside, came up to him and offered to help. "I can make the parrot fly," he promised. The king was skeptical. After all, the gardener had not received any formal education in medicine or in animal training. But he decided to play along. "It wouldn't hurt to try," he thought to himself.

The next morning, when the king woke up and opened his windows, he was astonished to see the parrot flying majestically in the sky. He sent for the gardener immediately. "How did you do it?" he inquired. "How did you train the parrot to fly so quickly?"

"It was fairly simple," explained the gardener. "All I had to do was cut off the branch the bird was sitting on."

Butterfly

ANCIENT SAGE ZHUANGZI dreamt one night that he was a butterfly. He fluttered around happily without a care in the world. His consciousness was that of a butterfly, and he knew nothing of the life of a human being. It was truly a great dream.

When he woke up in the morning, he was Zhuangzi again. But now he was confused. Was he really Zhuangzi who dreamt that he was a butterfly, or was he actually a butterfly dreaming that he is a human being called Zhuangzi? How could he know for sure?

List of Sources

1. This Will Change: Zen lore

2. One Taste: *Samguk Yusa*

3. The Poisoned Arrow: *Cula-Malunkyovada Sutta*

4. Forgetting: *Zhuangzi*

5. A Piggyback Ride: Zen lore

6. The Three Princesses: *Yoga Vasistha*

7. The Happy Fish: *Zhuangzi*

8. Blowing in the Wind: *The Platform Sutra*

9. The Acrobats: *Sedaka Sutta*

10. Hemp: *Payasi Sutta*

11. The Zen Master Who Killed a Cat: *The Gateless Gate*

12. The Runaway Horse: *Huainanzi*

13. Beautiful Flaws: Chinese folktale

14. A Handful of Mustard Seeds: *Therīgāthā*

15. Help the Grain: *Mencius*

16. The Nature of Scorpions: Zen lore

37. Empty Boat: *Zhuangzi*

38. Four Wives: Buddhist folktale

39. Can't get No Satisfaction: Chinese folktale

40. A Skull for a Pillow: *Zhuangzi*

41. The Wooden Idol: Zen lore

42. Hanging from a Cliff: Zen lore

43. The Servant's Dream: *Liezi*

44. The Mouse King: *Panchatantra*

45. The Hawk and the Clam: *Zhanguo ce*

46. The Gates of Heaven: Zen lore

47. The Magic Stick: Indian folktale

48. The Lazy Parrot: Indian folktale

49. Butterfly: *Zhuangzi*

WHAT DID YOU THINK OF

WISE TALES FROM THE EAST?

We hope that this book added meaning and quality to your life. If so, please share it with family, friends, and anyone else who may benefit from it.

Please feel free to add a review online or share your thoughts with us directly at prapanca_press@protonmail.com. Your feedback and support are valuable to us.

Thank you!